About the WOMEN OF OUR TIME™ *Series*

Today more than ever, children need role models whose lives can give them the inspiration and guidance to cope with a changing world. WOMEN OF OUR TIME, a series of biographies focusing on the lives of twentieth-century women, is the first such series designed specifically for the 7–11 age group. International in scope, these biographies cover a wide range of personalities—from historical figures to today's headliners—in such diverse fields as politics, the arts and sciences, athletics, and entertainment. Outstanding authors and illustrators present their subjects in a vividly anecdotal style, emphasizing the childhood and youth of each woman. More than a history lesson, the WOMEN OF OUR TIME books offer carefully documented life stories that will inform, entertain, and inspire the young people of our time.

BETTY FRIEDAN
A VOICE FOR WOMEN'S RIGHTS

BY MILTON MELTZER

Illustrated by Stephen Marchesi

VIKING KESTREL

VIKING KESTREL
Viking Penguin Inc., 40 West 23rd Street, New York, New York 10010, U.S.A.
Penguin Books Ltd, Harmondsworth, Middlesex, England
Penguin Books Australia Ltd, Ringwood, Victoria, Australia
Penguin Books Canada Limited, 2801 John Street, Markham, Ontario, Canada L3R 1B4
Penguin Books (N.Z.) Ltd, 182–190 Wairau Road, Auckland 10, New Zealand

First published in 1985 by Viking Penguin Inc.
Published simultaneously in Canada

"Women of Our Time" is a trademark of Viking Penguin Inc.

Library of Congress Cataloging in Publication Data
Meltzer, Milton,   Betty Friedan: a voice for women's rights.
(Women of our time)
Summary: Focuses on the childhood and youth of the writer, thinker,
and activist Betty Friedan.
1. Friedan, Betty—Juvenile literature.   2. Feminists—United States—Biography—
Juvenile literature. [1. Friedan, Betty. 2. Feminists] I. Marchesi, Stephen, ill.
II. Title.   III. Series.
HQ1413.F75M45 1985   305.4'2'0924 [B] [92]   85-40441   ISBN 0-670-80786-9

Printed in the United States of America by
The Book Press, Brattleboro, Vermont
Set in Garamond #3
1 2 3 4 5 89 88 87 86 85

Library of Congress Cataloging in Publication Data
Meltzer, Milton.   Betty Friedan: a voice for women's rights.

CONTENTS

1

I Want to *Do* Something!

She stood in front of the mirror and cried out, "Look, Ma! How tall I am!"

She was three and a half then, and for the first time she saw *herself:* Betty Goldstein.

Twelve years later she sat in the weed-filled, abandoned cemetery of her hometown, Peoria, Illinois, watching the sun go down. Tears filled her eyes as she thought about the girls and boys in her sophomore class at Central High. The sororities had pledged new members, and she was the only girl left out. That year her friends had started going out with older boys, but not one boy had dated her. Everyone was having a good time except Betty. At home, too, nothing she did seemed to be right. Her mother was always scolding her. Peoria—she hated it. I'll probably never get married. . . . No one wants me, she thought. Then she whispered the prayer she had made up to see her through these bad times: "I want a boy who will love me best, and I want a work to do."

The first request was never quite answered, for she had a troubled marriage that ended in divorce. But the second was fulfilled when the world came to know her as a founder of the modern movement for women's equality.

Betty was born on February 4, 1921, in the Proctor Hospital in Peoria. She was not a healthy baby, and for a while no one expected she would live long. Slowly she grew stronger, but her legs were so bowed that for three years she had to wear heavy braces to straighten them. In her first few winters she was battered by bronchitis or the flu. Her teeth came in wrong, and braces had to be fixed in her mouth. When she was eleven, the school discovered she could hardly see out of one eye; she had to wear glasses. "All in all," she said at seventeen, "I have not been well endowed physically, neither with health nor with beauty."

What nature did bless her with was an excellent mind. Her parents were bright people and well-to-do. Her father, Harry Goldstein, had come as a child with his family from Eastern Europe. They settled in St. Louis. One of nearly a dozen children, Harry was too poor to go on with school. At thirteen he wandered off on his own to Peoria, where he set up a street stand to sell collar buttons and to support himself. Later his earnings sent a brother through Harvard Law School.

Peoria was a city of 100,000, sitting on the bank of the Illinois River in the center of the state. By the early 1900s, it had become a major river and rail terminal, second in size only to Chicago. Thousands worked in its big plants, turning out tractors, whiskey, barrels, cordage, processing grains and curing meats. Young Harry Goldstein had the skills and energy to build a prosperous business in midtown. His jewelry store became a Tiffany of the Midwest, offering the rich the finest diamonds, silverware, china, and watches.

Harry fell in love with Miriam Horwitz. She was born in Peoria, but her family, too, had come over from Eastern Europe. Her father, a doctor, was chief of Peoria's public health service. Miriam was a graduate of Bradley, the local college. An attractive and able young woman, she liked to write and enjoyed her job as society editor of the local newspaper. But when she married Harry (he was forty, she was twenty-two), he insisted that she quit the paper to become a housewife and mother. In those times it was rare for a middle-class wife to work. People thought it strange if she did. Couldn't her husband support her? Or was something wrong with her? Reluctantly Miriam gave in. A year later, in 1921, Betty was born. Then came another girl, Amy, and a boy, Harry.

The Goldsteins lived in a comfortable red brick house, with large rooms and many windows, porches in front and back, and a big yard. It faced a park, and from Betty's bedroom windows upstairs she could see over the treetops to the meadows and woods beyond. At night she delighted in a sweeping view of the stars.

There was a maid to do the housework and a man to drive the family car. Betty's father rarely took a vacation, working long hours six days a week. He sent the family up to Wisconsin or Minnesota for summer holidays. Breakfast and supper were the times he always saved for his children. They got up at seven and walked with him in the park before breakfast. When she was little, Betty took salt along in the hope of putting some on the tail of a robin so she could catch it. At supper, as at every meal, there was a tall glass of milk to down. Disgusting. And she hated the naps she was forced to take each afternoon when she was little. She'd just lie there, making up stories and letting her wild imagination roam.

With her sister, Amy, she was always making up

games. "We'd race to see who'd get dressed first, and
while we washed, we'd pretend the bathroom floor
and the inside of the tub were the ocean and the rim
of the bathtub was our boat. We had to walk all the
way around the rim and not fall off. We made up
poems that no one could understand but us, because
they were in a private language."

At six Betty went to Whittier School. She learned
easily to read and write and do arithmetic. Because
she was so quick, they skipped her in second grade
and then again in the fourth grade. Here she made

the friends she'd stay with through elementary school. She never forgot their names—Marian, Otty, Nancy, Billy, Bob, Ned, Paul, Jimmy. After school they took dancing classes; Betty was clumsy and hated it. Finally she got her mother to let her switch to dramatic classes. She loved rehearsing parts and seeing the professional shows that now and then came to Peoria.

Soon her friends were calling her "Bookworm." She could never get enough to read. Whenever anyone asked her what she wanted for Christmas or her birthday, she'd say, "Books!" She read one or two almost every day. She told herself, I'll be a librarian when I grow up—then I'll always be close to books. The worst punishment her mother could think of was to forbid her to read for a week. Then, of course, she would sneak a book under her blanket at night and read by flashlight.

Her gang's favorite game was "Dressup." They raided their mothers' collections of old dresses and scarves and hats and coats stored in the attic and made themselves up into beautiful and elegant princesses, heiresses, movie stars. Or they borrowed ideas from the mysteries they all swapped and would imitate Nancy Drew's adventures. Betty always played the villain as they pulled down the shades and tapped the walls for secret passages. In class they passed notes to each other in secret codes.

When the girls began pairing off with boys, Betty

would decide she "liked" this one or that because he "liked" her. They started a club called the "JFF" (Just For Fun) and on Friday nights played Post Office or Hide in the Dark. To make school more interesting, Betty started the Baddy Baddy Club. At her signal the kids would suddenly drop their books on the floor or cough violently or chew gum loudly in rhythm. Finally the principal called her in and said, "You've got a talent for leadership, Betty, but why do you use it to do harm? I hope you find a way to use it wisely." She left his office in tears. The next year, her last at Whittier, she behaved herself, even though it wasn't as much fun.

With junior high came the chance to act in school plays. Wanting even more of drama, she joined a neighborhood children's theater and made up skits to perform in home room programs. She wrote for the school paper, *The Reflector,* and went to the weekly basketball games in the winter. On Saturday nights her crowd would meet at somebody's house or go to a dance. She got a few B's in her classes but still collected mostly A's.

Moving on to Central High, she began the worst time of her school life. That year every girl but Betty was pledged by a sorority. These clubs of girls limited their membership. They chose the ones they wanted on the basis of race and religion. And more—you had to have the right background, the right looks, the right style. Betty wasn't an attractive girl, and her long nose had sometimes been the target of crude jokes. Still, up to now, her appearance and the fact that she was Jewish hadn't mattered to her friends. In high school it suddenly mattered. The girls from well-to-do families like her own lumped Jews with blacks and working-class kids who lived on "the wrong side of town."

Betty's parents had feared this might happen in high school, when serious dating began, for they had found this separation to be true in their own social life. Jews were a tiny minority in Peoria. Her father said non-Jews friendly to him during business hours wouldn't speak to him after sundown. Gentiles kept Jews out of their country club and out of their homes.

At school there were no other Jewish girls or boys of Betty's age to make a crowd of their own. She felt all alone now. That she was at the top of her class in almost every subject didn't help her any. She buried herself in reading. She went to the town library every Saturday and carried home a stack of books. "Don't do that," her father said. "Five books at a time is enough! It doesn't look nice for a girl to be so bookish." Yet he was proud of her; he kept the poems she wrote in his safe.

In class she began to pretend she wasn't so bright. She tried not to raise her hand so often. Maybe that would make her more popular. A fine physics student, she pretended the experiments were too hard. She did the math for the athletes' lab reports and got them to do her wiring and splicing. It made no difference. She was still left out. "I felt terribly alone," she said, "so self-conscious, and miserable."

The few times she had dates the boys were rejects, outsiders. She began to think there was something wrong when people who were Jewish or black or poor were swept to one side as though they didn't count. She herself, she realized, had hardly been aware of the working people who lived below the hill. Most of their kids didn't finish high school, and few dreamed of going to college.

At night Betty would look out at the park from her bedroom, think of the others all having a good time, and cry. Then one night she decided to get rid of her misery. There are two ways to be a success in high school, she told herself. Either be very popular or be very prominent in school affairs. Since she could never be the first, she would try to be the second.

So when her junior year began, she made herself too busy to waste time feeling sorry for herself. She took five hard subjects—chemistry, algebra, Latin, French, and English. Enthralled with chemistry, Betty read a biography of Marie Curie, the woman who won two Nobel prizes for her scientific research. I'd like to do something like that, she thought—only to be told by her teacher that there was no future for a girl in science. Better plan on being a doctor's receptionist or a lab technician, the teacher advised.

Her English teacher, Miss Crowder, proved to be the best she ever had. From her, Betty learned to read far more widely and thoughtfully. She came to enjoy poetry and essays as well as fiction. She wrote book reviews for *Opinion,* the school newspaper, and a column called "Cabbages and Kings." In the school essay contest on "Why I Am Proud to Be an American," she won first prize.

The sororities stayed closed to her. But she was accepted by other school clubs. That spring she played a tough old woman in the junior class play, and staged her own reading of Emily Dickinson's poems. Although she had won several new friends, she warned herself not to get too close to anyone. She didn't want to be hurt again.

Her junior year was much better than her sophomore, except that as she grew a bit older, she became more aware of trouble at home. Sometimes she would wake in the night to hear angry voices coming from her parents' room. They quarreled bitterly over money. It was 1938 now, and the Great Depression had gone on for years. Her father's business, like so many others, was doing poorly. The family had to cut down on living expenses. No maid, no driver, no luxuries. But her mother couldn't seem to accept these facts. She ran up big bills on her charge accounts. When she got

desperate about paying them on her reduced allowance, she gambled in the hope of making up the money. She always lost and then had to face her husband's terrible temper when the bills came due. What made it worse was Miriam's feeling of superiority to her husband. She was a native-born American, embarrassed by an immigrant husband, who had no formal education. She showed it in the way she bossed him around. It triggered his terrible temper. He got even with her when she had to come to him in trouble.

Betty saw that her mother was unhappy. It puzzled her. Unlike herself, her mother was good-looking and dressed beautifully. Miriam busied herself teaching Sunday school, volunteering for the Community Chest, for Hadassah, for the Temple Sisterhood. She played golf and bridge. But she demanded that everyone do everything perfectly. Nothing that Betty or anyone else in the family did was good enough for her. What could make such a capable woman with a successful husband and three children so dissatisfied with life? Whatever it was, it came out in anger against her husband and nagging of her children.

The family fights upset Betty, frightened her. She tried to bury her feeling by keeping herself very busy. When the senior year began, she started a literary magazine with a few other students. She worked hard day and night to make *Tide* the best of its kind. It was a triumph to raise the money to pay the printer and

12

a joy to take part in the editorial meetings where they hatched ideas, corrected proofs, pasted up the dummy. When *Tide* finally came out, it was an instant success.

The drama still held her fast. She directed a play and, in the senior class production of *Jane Eyre,* she played the madwoman. A small part, but when she walked onstage and gave a horrible insane laugh, it scared the audience so deliciously that they gave her a big hand as she exited.

It was fun being a senior and doing so many things people liked and being looked up to. As the term ended, she wrote a long essay about reaching seventeen. "I want my life to be full of beauty," she said, "and I want to create beauty, ... I want to fall in love and be loved and be needed by someone. I want to have children.

"I know this," she went on. "I don't want to marry a man and keep house for him and be the mother of his children and nothing else. I want to *do* something with my life. I want success and fame."

2

Campus Life

What college shall I go to? That question looms large in the last years of high school. That is, if you are lucky enough to have parents who can manage to send you. Betty applied to several colleges: her record was so good they all accepted her. She chose Smith, an Ivy League women's college in a beautiful part of western Massachusetts. She wanted to get far away from Peoria and an unhappy family. And Smith promised a first-rate education. She didn't yet know what she wanted to be. Her studies had all been easy for her, but what could she do best? Become a psychologist and study human emotions, human relations? That had always fascinated her. "Whatever I do," she said then, "I want to write, but to be able to write, I must live first."

She found college vastly different from high school. In Peoria she had been one of the best and brightest students. At Smith there were lots of such girls. She couldn't shine so easily in her classes. But then the keen competition made her work harder and do better.

She found anti-Semitism again at Smith. There were relatively few Jewish students on campus. Many private schools and colleges in those days refused Jews altogether. Or at best they used a quota system to reduce the number of "those people." They gave professorships to only a handful of Jews.

Socially, Jews might be outsiders; still, Betty found she was liked for what she was and what she was good at. She made friends among the faculty, men as well as women. She learned much from Kurt Koffka, one of the leading psychologists. Encouraged by him, she decided to make psychology her major field of study.

Her other talents—or lack of them—persisted. She never could do well in sports. Basketball, volleyball, softball, tennis—a flop at all of them. Exercise without a ball was her speed. She liked to hike and explore strange places. Writing—that interest found many outlets. In a history seminar she tracked original sources

Susan B. Anthony
Elizabeth Cady Stanton
Margaret Fuller

to prepare a paper on the French Revolution. It excited her that the ideas enlightened men and women proclaimed—liberty, equality, fraternity—could ignite a revolution.

Even in high school she had begun to explore the power of ideas. One of her essays questioned whether the hateful ideas of Hitler could take root in the democratic soil of America. Back then the girls sat around at bull sessions and talked about finding boyfriends and getting married. At Smith you could talk not only

Charlotte Perkins Gilman

Lucy Stone

Abraham Lincoln

about yourself but about what was going on in the world.

Later, however, Betty realized nothing was ever said, in class or out, about women and their history. Forgotten were the stories of the great American women of the past: Margaret Fuller, Elizabeth Cady Stanton, Lucy Stone, Susan B. Anthony, Charlotte Perkins Gilman. It was as though they had never existed. Not even for this women's college!

When Betty thought of heroic figures, it was men who came to mind. Abraham Lincoln was her earliest

17

idol, partly because he had lived in her state, Illinois, and she had grown up on the legend of the Great Emancipator. It was in her own hometown in 1854 that Lincoln made his first public attack on slavery. Later Betty learned that way back in 1836 Lincoln said that all women should have the right to vote. They paid taxes, didn't they, so why shouldn't they vote? Even that early he stood with the pioneers of the women's rights movement.

On campus there was a chapter of the American Student Union. Formed in the mid-1930s, it took a stand against the growing danger of wars ignited by the dictators, Hitler of Germany and Mussolini of Italy. The members put out a paper called *Focus*. It printed some of Betty's poems and a review she wrote of John Steinbeck's new novel about the migrant workers, *The Grapes of Wrath*. She hailed it as "a fiery document of protest and compassion."

Finding no literary magazine at Smith, Betty helped start the *Smith College Monthly*. It aimed to reflect the thinking of students of all opinions. Betty contributed short stories, poems, and essays. When Hitler's armies began invading Western Europe, her editorial warned that if he wasn't stopped, his kind of brutal dictatorship could come to the United States, too.

By her junior year Betty was a campus celebrity. She became the editor-in-chief of the college's newspaper, *SCAN*. She put it out twice a week, with a huge staff of eighty girls. In her editorials she took up many issues, from encouraging workers on the campus to join a union, to developing an exposé of a secret society. Made up mostly of wealthy Eastern girls, the snobbish group dominated campus life, pulling all the strings behind the scenes. Betty's investigating reporters found evidence to prove their case. But before *SCAN* could print it, the college president got word of what was up. He threatened to expel the reporters if the story wasn't killed. Under great pressure the staff agreed to drop the exposé; Betty ran a blank page in the next issue stamped: CENSORED.

At Smith Betty gradually lost her painful shyness with boys. Dating was still a problem. But that was true for most students at a women's college, where no men appeared except perhaps on weekends. Nevertheless she loved the life at Smith. Health—her own and her father's—was her only worry. Asthma had begun to bother her in her freshman year. In her junior year, while skiing, she had a savage attack. The breathing disorder—wheezing, coughing, tightness of the chest—came on so violently it collapsed a lung. Her friends rushed her to the college infirmary, fearing she would die. She recovered slowly, but asthma hounded her from then on. Her father fell ill too. His heart trouble got so bad that Betty's mother had to take charge of his business.

Twice, when the campus shut down for the summer, Betty went off on special projects. The first time, she worked in Iowa with a refugee from Hitler's Germany, the eminent psychologist Kurt Lewin. The second time, she was sent by her economics professor to the Highlander Folk School in Tennessee. He thought she needed to learn something about the working people, mostly Southerners, who came to Highlander to study labor history and union organization. The six weeks were packed with lessons in labor journalism and public speaking, skills she did not then know she would put to use very soon.

In June 1942 Betty was graduated from Smith. The college years had made her feel responsible for her own fate. And they had given her a deep concern for injustice, and an awareness of the power of people to make the world better. Her honors were many: election to Phi Beta Kappa and Sigma Xi—societies of the best scholars—a bachelor's degree summa cum laude, and a fellowship to go on to graduate study of psychology at the University of California in Berkeley. She felt bad when her father refused to attend the ceremony. He pleaded illness, but added that if he did show up, Betty would be ashamed of him.

Although she had been a "big woman on campus" at Smith, Betty panicked as she faced going to Berkeley for her master's degree. Her fear came out in renewed bouts of asthma. Once started, however, she found Berkeley less demanding than Smith. It was easy to do well there, and when the year ended she was offered a fellowship to work on a doctoral program.

For reasons she didn't quite understand, she refused the grant. Was laboratory research what she really wanted? Wouldn't she rather be a doer than a theorist? Then, too, the country was caught up in the fever of World War II, and she wanted to do her part. She volunteered for Red Cross work overseas, but was turned down. She had been happiest when working on the college newspaper at Smith. Maybe writing was what she was meant to do.

She left Berkeley in 1943 and moved to New York. Together with a few Smith classmates she shared an apartment in the Greenwich Village neighborhood. She made the rounds of newspaper offices. "No job here," said one editor, "but I hear there's an opening in a news agency that services the labor press." So Betty applied and was given a job left open by a woman who'd moved to the Washington office. Betty was on her way now—a real job in the real world.

3

Reporter

Labor reporter. No glamour job. It meant low wages, long hours, hard work. But it was work Betty loved and did gladly. Federated Press had a small staff, with news bureaus in New York and Washington and correspondents in several major cities. Her editor told her what news to cover, or Betty came up with her own ideas. She fished eagerly for stories no one else had thought of. When she hooked a good one, she'd hang on relentlessly, searching for the facts and interviewing people who knew them. More than once the editor had to bully Betty into wrapping the story up in a hurry because she had forgotten the deadline.

The war ended and soldiers coming home asked for their old jobs back. Betty was bumped from the labor news service by a returning veteran. It wasn't easy to find a new job with millions of GIs looking for work. Several women she knew had jobs as researchers at the *Time* and *Life* magazines, and she applied there. She didn't get a job, but she wasn't really sorry. For no matter how good the women were—and often *they* wrote the stories the men signed—women were never promoted to writers or editors.

Soon she found a job with a trade union newspaper read by a million electrical workers. Again the pay was small and the hours long. The union liked her reporting, though they could see she had never worked in a factory but was a middle-class woman. She bubbled over with energy, talked in spurts, rarely finishing a sentence, her mind racing so fast the words couldn't keep up with it. She visited factories that made all sorts of electrical products. Her job was to get the story of how the workers lived and what they hoped for. "What are your skills?" she'd ask. "What pay do you earn? Is it enough to take care of yourself and your family?" Once she got them talking, they would often tell her all sorts of things about their lives on the job and at home. She began to understand, to feel what a worker's life was like.

Her writing improved. The stories had to be simple, clear, direct. She was forced to give up the more elaborate literary style of her Smith days. Reporting the everyday lives of people so different from herself broadened her range and sharpened her skills.

In those postwar years the unions often had to strike for better wages and working conditions. Betty covered the picket lines, the union rallies, the bargaining between management and labor. Every other week, back from the field, she and her managing editor went down to the grubby printshop to "put the paper to bed." They stayed until 3:00 A.M. to check

the first copies off press. "It was no nine-to-five job, but a cause," she said. "Our pay was never more than what the worker on the line got."

. From the beginning the union carried on a fight to win equality for women workers. Betty learned the companies did not give women the same rate of pay as the men for the same work. Nor did they give women the chance to work at all jobs in the plant. She saw that when the soldiers came marching home, the women had to quit their jobs to make way for them. Betty did many stories about the unfair treatment women got. And then she wrote a forty-page pamphlet for the union to explain how less pay for women undermined the men's pay scale. That, in turn, meant greater profits for the companies and less money for the workers.

She tried to make men understand why they ought to get together with women to fight the double standard. When women suffered unequal treatment, it hurt men, too. She began to see that women workers faced other problems—the need for day nurseries to care for their children while they worked, for maternity leave with pay, for health protection, for leadership training.

It was through another labor reporter that Betty met Carl Friedan. He had come back from running a soldier show in Europe to start a summer theater in New Jersey. His best friend told him he knew a nice girl with an apartment. (There was a bad housing shortage after the war.) Betty's group in Greenwich Village had broken up as the other women married. She had found a small apartment in the basement of a house on the Upper West Side of New York City. Carl brought her an apple, and the courtship began. In 1947 they were married. A year later they had their first child, Daniel.

So she had a man and a family and a home. Nobody had to tell a woman that was what she wanted. But a new twist to that message began hitting women from all sides. Domestic bliss was the only thing a woman should want, it said. To pursue a career was to risk that happiness.

The stories in the women's magazines all said that girls with supposedly glamorous jobs were really miserable—until they saw the light and quit to marry the man. To fulfill herself a girl had to escape the trap of work and flee to that dream house in the suburbs. Forget about having a career, the message went. Just "be" a woman and raise a family—the bigger the better. Why compete for a job? Why take on the hard work of a man's world? No need to risk failure or to make men resent you.

This sounded right to Betty, as it did to millions of middle-class girls. Of course, it meant your man had to earn enough to support a family. For women working at routine jobs in factories, stores, and offices, there was no such choice. They *had* to work to help put food on the table and pay the rent and buy the clothing.

Betty took a maternity leave for a year so she could stay at home and nurse her baby. When she went back to her job, much of her money went to pay for someone to care for the child and the apartment. Carl's income from advertising and public relations work was not steady, and though her pay was low, it was needed. When her son was about three, she read of a new garden apartment community in Queens called Parkway Village. It was built for families working for the United Nations headquarters in New York. But it made room for some war veterans and their families. Best of all, it had a cooperative nursery school.

The babies, the bottles, the diapering, the cooking, the carriage-wheeling, the barbecue, the playground—she found it all more satisfying than the "career" where you knew you wouldn't get anywhere. Yet she went on working, the idea of a career still driving her, even though the men in the office didn't take a woman reporter seriously. At home, however, she was *necessary*. She was the boss—the mother—and weren't the magazines telling her this was the real career? Other mothers let her know they disapproved of a woman who went on working while she still had children to raise.

She thought her conflict was ended when she left

her job. The union decided to cut the paper's staff, and, pregnant again, with Jonathan, she offered to quit so another reporter, a man, could stay on. It was a relief not to go out to work and not to feel guilty about it. She took a special delight in the early years of her children. They were "surprising undeserved gifts." Many years later she could still recall how each one looked in the delivery room, "how Jonathan as a flannel-wrapped newborn kicked with that lusty energy he still has, and I can see him at three in the cowboy hat he never took off, getting off his little horse-on-wheels to climb into my lap."

But soon she grew restless, wanting to do something besides housework and raising babies. She would keep her skill up by writing for the Parkway Village paper. That wasn't enough. So, with a friend, she worked up an article in the form of a debate. Her friend wrote the side called, "I Want to Stay Home with My Kids." Betty took the other side, "I'd Rather Work." They got a literary agent to read it. She liked it and placed it in *Charm* magazine.

Success! It got the ball rolling. Betty saw she could stay at home and still work as a writer. She chose subjects that wouldn't take her far from family. Stories of a great dress designer, of an actress, of other successful people. A sketch of the suburban dream house. Another of a cooperative community. The ideas came easily, but the work was hard. It took about a month to do the research and writing. She could not manage more than four or five pieces a year, what with managing home and family, too.

The Friedans made ends meet, but just barely. Betty earned enough to pay for a part-time housekeeper so she could go on writing. If an article was turned down, she got the blues until her agent sold it to another magazine. Free-lancing is always uncertain and risky.

With a second child, and a third—Emily—to come, the Friedans decided it would be cheaper to find an old house in the country. They rented a stone barn in Sneden's Landing up in Rockland County, New York, not far from the city. It was too costly to heat; they kept the thermostat so low that Betty typed with gloves on.

One day Betty met a woman scientist who worked at the Lamont Geological Survey nearby. She told Betty of a new discovery in the earth's core that indicated another ice age might descend on the earth. Excited by how they discovered this, Betty wrote an article which *Harper's* published as the cover story and *Reader's Digest* reprinted. An editor of the Norton publishing house liked the piece and asked Betty to develop it into a book. She shied away, not confident enough to tackle so big an enterprise.

It was 1956. Word came that next year Betty's class at Smith would hold its fifteenth reunion. She was asked to prepare a questionnaire for members of the class. What were their experiences and feelings fifteen years after leaving Smith? Betty took it on, thinking she would get a magazine article out of it. She had never gone to a class reunion before because she found it hard to face the other women. What had she done with her life? She wasn't great, she wasn't famous, she couldn't see around the next corner of life. My brilliant career, she thought, has come to very little in my midthirties.

She put a tremendous effort into the task, far more than was called for. Her questions went below the quiet surface of her classmates' lives. She thought the answers would show that a good education did not keep women from fitting into their roles as housewives. Betty wanted to believe that herself, to end the doubt gnawing at the back of her own mind.

When the answers came in, they astonished her. She had discovered, as she called it, "the problem that has no name."

4

The Problem That Has No Name

What had she discovered?

That there was something very wrong about the way women were trying to live their lives.

The answers given by 200 classmates to her questions showed there was a great split between the reality of their lives and the image they were trying to fit. These suburban housewives thought they had everything. Husbands climbing the ladder of success. Children in good schools. A daughter taking ballet classes. A son on the basketball team. All the modern household appliances. And didn't all the magazines they read in the beauty parlor praise the delights of being wife and mother? Yet Betty's classmates were asking, "Is this all? Is there nothing else to my life?"

What they asked was what Betty had begun to sense in her own life. As a wife and mother of three small children she was feeling guilty, and therefore halfhearted, about using her abilities and education to do writing that took her away from home. Now she knew a great many of her classmates felt as she did.

I do have a story to tell, she said, and sat down to write it. She sent it to *McCall's* magazine. It was turned down. The women on the staff confided that *they* liked it; the male editor didn't. The *Ladies' Home Journal* took it, but rewrote it to say exactly the opposite. Betty withdrew the article. She began to do more research. She talked to child guidance experts, to psychologists, to guidance counselors. She interviewed many more women who had gone to other colleges, and women who lived in the suburbs. She added more material to her piece. Then *Redbook* looked at it and told her only "sick" women would identify with it. Betty realized the women's magazines did not want to print what she had discovered because it went against everything they stood for.

Discouraged, she went to a meeting of magazine writers. She heard a man talk about the thrill of writing his first book after years of free-lance magazine work.

On the way out she thought, if he can do it, so can I! When she got home she called her agent and said, "I've got this great idea! Why don't I build that article into a book?" Her agent sent her to Norton, who had once asked her for a book on the ice age. This "problem that has no name," they said, "sounds important. You're on to something. Do it." And they gave her $1000 to get started.

Betty settled in to work. She thought the book would take her a year to write. It took five years, demanding wide research and hard thinking to figure out why this had happened to women and what it was doing to them. All the bits and pieces of her own life began to come together.

She worked at home in the rambling old Victorian house they had moved into on the Hudson River. She spread her notes and papers and books all over the dining room table. And when the family ate, she stuffed the litter under the china closet. Sometimes she worked in an office in the city which her husband shared with a friend. Then she heard that the New York Public Library had opened a special work room for writers who needed peace and quiet. It was a godsend. She took a bus into the city from Rockland County three days a week and wrote at her desk in the library.

She continued to interview women, to talk with experts, to test her ideas against theirs. She went back over the files of women's magazines for the past fifteen

years to see what they told their readers, how they influenced them. And gradually she unraveled what she called the feminine mystique. A mystique is a group of ideas or beliefs clustered around an object or a person; in this case, around women. It is supposed to provide a special value or meaning. And it implies something mysterious, something with magical powers.

"The problem that has no name" lay buried, unspoken, for many years in the minds of American women, she wrote in her book. "It was a strange stirring, a sense of dissatisfaction. For more than fifteen years there was no word of this yearning in the millions of words written about women, for women, in all the columns, books, and articles by experts telling women their role was to seek fulfillment as wives and mothers. Over and over, women heard they "could desire no greater destiny than to glory in their own femininity." This was the feminine mystique.

Experts, she wrote, told women "how to catch a man and keep him, how to breastfeed children and handle their toilet training, how to cope with sibling rivalry and adolescent rebellion; how to buy a dishwasher, bake bread, cook gourmet snails, and build a swimming pool with their own hands; how to dress, look, and act more feminine and make marriage more exciting; how to keep their husbands from dying young and their sons from growing into delinquents. They

36

were taught to pity the neurotic, unfeminine, unhappy women who wanted to be poets or physicists or presidents. They learned that truly feminine women do not want careers, higher education, political rights— the independence and the opportunities that the old-fashioned feminists fought for. . . . All they had to do was devote their lives from earliest girlhood to finding a husband and bearing children."

Then why were all these women unhappy? Why this groping, this searching going on in their minds? It wasn't easy for them to put it into words because they struggled with it alone. They were afraid to admit they were asking themselves the silent question, "Is this all?"

The experts kept tracing all the emotional problems and disappointments of children and men back to Mother. And Mother, they said, had been spoiled by education and freedom, by her striving for a career and independence and equality with men. *That* was what made American women unfeminine.

Yet when Betty talked with women, they said, "I feel empty somehow," or "useless," or "incomplete." To blot out the feeling they took pills or redecorated the house or moved to a better neighborhood. Sometimes women went to their doctor with symptoms they couldn't describe: I'm always tired. . . . I get so angry with the kids it scares me. . . . I feel like crying without any reason. . . .

Betty learned it took some women half a lifetime before they found the courage to admit it was not enough to be a wife and mother because they were human beings, themselves. They couldn't live through their husbands and children. They had to find their own fulfillment as individuals.

What was the answer? In the last chapter of her book, *The Feminine Mystique,* Betty tried to suggest it. First of all, a woman should listen to her own voice. Once she faces the problem and asks, "What do I want to do?" she begins to find her own answers. Betty gave many kinds of answers picked up from women she interviewed. She concluded that "the only way for a woman, as for a man, to find herself, to know herself as a person, is by creative work of her own." Not just any job to fill in time. But a job "she can take seriously as part of her life plan, work in which she can grow as part of society." Even if a woman does not have to work to eat, Betty said, "she can find identity only in work that is of real value to society— work for which, usually, our society pays. Being paid is, of course, more than a reward—it implies a definite commitment."

What women need, she said, is education, more education, reeducation. Education that will take them out of themselves and into the mainstream of men's activities.

There were risks in doing this. Some husbands refused to let their wives work or go back to school. Other housewives resented the woman who had a life of her own. And it took a strong will to move out of this trap. "Ambition," like "career," had been made a dirty word by the feminine mystique. But for women who suffered and solved the problem that has no name, to fulfill this ambition, to have a sense of achievement, was "to find a missing piece in the puzzle of their lives." The money they earned often was a help to the family. But great, too, was "the sense of being complete and feeling a part of the world."

5

It Changed Their Lives

Betty was years late in completing her book. Tired of waiting for it, the Norton people had lost their enthusiasm. They printed only 3000 copies in 1963, expecting to take a small loss on the book. But Betty knew she had something big and important to say. She got Norton to hire a free-lance publicity woman to promote the book, then went out herself on television programs and radio talk shows.

The Feminine Mystique took off. The first women who read it couldn't stop talking about it. By word of mouth, the sales climbed higher and higher. The very women's magazines whose mystique she was challenging paid to print long excerpts from the book. And millions more read its message. When a paperback edition came out, sales climbed to one, two, and then three million copies. Within a few years the book was translated into thirteen languages.

Life magazine called it "an angry, thoroughly documented book that in one way or another is going to provoke the daylights out of everyone who reads it." The *Washington Post* said, "It deserves cheers for daring women to take a more intelligent approach to life and work." One reviewer wrote that the book shows "something is rotten in the current state of American womanhood." Friedan tells the reader "what it is, why it is, and what to do about it."

In the weeks and months after the book appeared, Betty got ample proof that she was not alone. The letters that poured in showed what a relief it was for women to have their questions put into words. After reading those words, some women began to make changes in their lives almost at once. But there were angry letters, too, attacking Betty as a destroyer of the family, an enemy of motherhood. The book was a threat to women whose hidden feelings were too painful for them to examine.

Betty had not set out consciously to start a revolution. But the book changed her life as a woman and as a writer, and other women told her it changed theirs. A Florida mother of four wrote: "I have been trying for years to tell my husband of my need to do something to find myself, to have a purpose. All I've ever achieved was to end up feeling guilty about wanting to be more than a housewife and mother." And a woman from Massachusetts: "I have for the past ten years now been asking myself, 'Is this all there is to life?' I am a housewife and mother of five children. I have a very poor education. I am thirty-eight years old, and if this is all there is for me to look forward to, I don't want to go on."

From a twenty-six-year-old mother of three children in Michigan: "Here I am! I feel like an appliance. I want to live. I want more education and a chance to compete in this world. My brain seems dead, and I am nothing but a parasite."

From Connecticut came this letter: "Did God ordain woman's weakness? For the benefit of my fellow Catholics, the great saints who have been women were rarely those who just stayed home and did the wash. In fact, I can't name one. But I can name Joan of Arc, Saint Bridget of Sweden, Saint Teresa of Avila, the parables of Mary and Martha. . . . All this concerns me because I've got two daughters who are at least as intelligent and creative as their brothers."

Years later historians would agree that among the voices that helped create an atmosphere favorable to women's rights, none was more influential than Betty

Friedan's book *The Feminine Mystique*. Her book appeared just at that time when nearly half of all the women in the United States were already working outside the home to help pay the bills—and feeling guilty about it. They made the connection between their lives and what Betty said. Her book was the first of many to make a powerful case for women's equality.

Like most people, Betty wanted to be known, to be recognized. So did her husband. When her book was published, Carl liked it and tried to help promote it. But when it shot up to the best-seller list and her name appeared everywhere, it was hard for him to take it. A marriage that had been stormy from the beginning began to fall apart. Carl didn't relish being "Mr. Betty Friedan." Whatever had made their marriage rocky became worse. In 1969, after twenty-two years of marriage, they divorced.

6

Women Are People

There are some books that are like a revelation. They go straight to the reader's heart. So it was with Betty's book. It touched the lives of untold thousands of women and somehow changed them. Defeats or disappointments that women had once dismissed as personal, trivial, or their own fault, they now felt keenly as injustices. That is, they now saw their lives as shaped by social conditions. Women had been deprived of a chance to realize their dreams by a society that denied their equality with men.

But how could they do something about it? There

was no women's movement to express their political discontent. It was about to be born, created out of the same struggle for equality that powered the civil rights movement. When Betty's book appeared in 1963, the country was in the midst of a great crusade for civil rights. Years before, blacks in the South had begun the fight to end racial segregation and discrimination. Their protests soon spread to Northern cities as whites joined with blacks in demonstrations for the right to vote and an end to discrimination in jobs, housing, education, social services. And then it moved to the schools and colleges. In the summer of 1963 hundreds of young people journeyed South to help blacks fight for their rights as citizens and their dignity as human beings.

To cement those rights into law, the Congress banned race discrimination—that was the main drive. And it banned sex discrimination in employment, too. Perhaps because the politicians were becoming dimly aware of the potential of the women's vote out there. A federal agency was set up to enforce the act. But from the start it was clear that the Equal Employment Opportunity Commission (EEOC) would focus on racial discrimination. Women's rights? That would be put aside for another time.

In June 1966, when the law had been on the books awhile, Betty went to Washington to see what was being done about sex discrimination. She learned that thousands of women in factories and offices had filed complaints, complaints that employers didn't even bother to deny. But the EEOC was doing nothing to enforce the law.

President Lyndon B. Johnson had actually disbanded the National Commission on the Status of Women after it made its report. Only the fifty state EEOCs continued. But they were dependent on governors for their jobs. They were timid; they had no power to act.

A female EEOC lawyer asked Betty into her office, closed the door, and with tears in her eyes said, "Betty, you've got to do something. You're the only one who can. You have to start a national organization to fight for women, like the civil rights movement for the blacks."

Betty was taken aback. She'd never joined any women's groups. She had no patience for that kind of thing. She was a writer, a loner. Besides, why didn't the unions do it? Or the women's organizations that had been around for years?

She learned that all those state EEOCs were to meet soon in Washington. Betty decided to report on that meeting.

And that's where it began. On her first night in Washington Betty invited a dozen women to her hotel room. They talked about what could be done to enforce the law against discrimination. But few seemed

ready for anything as "radical" as a civil rights movement for women. They agreed on only one thing. At tomorrow's EEOC meeting they would insist on a resolution demanding the enforcement of the law.

What happened the next day enraged them. They were told that the conference had no power to take any action, even to pass a resolution, on sex discrimination! You can just talk, in other words, and go home.

Fighting mad, the small group of women who had failed to get action on the floor met with Betty at lunch. They were ready to discuss forming the organization Betty now saw was needed. At the table she began scribbling on a paper napkin the statement of purpose the new National Organization of Women (NOW) would soon adopt.

It was no easy step for Betty to take. Later she wrote: "Yes, we knew what we were doing. We couldn't possibly know where it would lead, but we knew what had to be done. But why me, why us? Who wants to take the responsibility, to commit oneself to carry it through, and risk being laughed at, getting people mad at you, maybe getting fired?" Those who started NOW were all "reluctant heroines," she said.

At first with only thirty-two founding members, NOW set out to change the conditions that denied women their right to become fully human. NOW drew up a Bill of Rights for Women and called for passage of the Equal Rights Amendment (ERA) to the Constitution. It pledged "to take action to bring women into full participation in the mainstream of American society now, exercising all the privileges and responsibilities thereof in truly equal partnership with men."

Elected the first president of NOW, Betty made the movement her full-time work. Widely known as an author, she became widely known as an activist. She petitioned the President for legislation to help women achieve first-class citizenship. She fought to put teeth into the Civil Rights Act and guts into the EEOC. She sat in at restaurants to protest their males-only rules. She spoke out against newspaper "help wanted" ads that separated jobs by sex, against political parties that had no room for women's rights in their platforms, against textbook publishers who left out women's part in history. She lobbied for child care centers, for equal employment opportunities, for ERA.

In those early years of NOW, Betty's talents were badly needed. She gave the mass media what they always look for—the star image, an individual they can focus on, the one who projects the ideas of a whole movement. She found her strength slowly, learning to conduct meetings and rallies, to pull together disagreeing groups, to get things *done*. Her busy imagination came up with great ideas for ways to win public attention and advance the cause. And in that new phase of women's self-development she was superb. "Consciousness raising," they called it, when women met in small groups to talk about their needs and desires and fears and doubts and to give one another strength and courage and a sense of sisterhood. She spoke hundreds of times all across the country, and NOW chapters sprang up wherever she went. Her husky voice was heard everywhere. "So distinctive," said one reporter, "it sounded like tires on a gravel driveway."

One of Betty's co-workers in the early feminist movement described her this way: "She sweeps through meetings, telephone calls, dinners and speeches with frantic bursts of energy as if each day might be her last. Everything is in motion, not just her words, which come so fast she seems to ignore the necessity of breathing. Her hands gesticulate, wave, flail. Her eyes are deep, dark, charged, and violent as her language. Her nose is long, her hair, despite patient attention at the beauty parlor, often askew. Nothing fits the accepted model of beauty. Yet she exerts a powerful, haunting attractiveness—that special combustion that lights up a few rare individuals interacting with their audience."

By the early 1970s women had formed several other organizations devoted to pressing for equality. Betty was one of the leaders of the National Women's Political Caucus. Women like Gloria Steinen, Bella Abzug,

Jane Fonda, and feminist men like Alan Alda shared in the common goal of trying to open politics to more women. The Women's Equity Action League (WEAL) focused on three areas of discrimination: jobs, education, and taxes. *Ms* magazine, founded in 1971, gave women a growing feminist voice that won national readership. Groups of radical women moved to the extreme of separating themselves from men, calling them the enemy. Men, Betty kept saying, are not the enemy; they're fellow victims. But all the groups were united on a core set of demands: an end to job discrimination, the creation of child-care centers, and most important of all, an end to the treatment of women not as individuals but as sex objects or servants. By the end of the 1970s their cause had won the attention and support of government, the college campuses, the mass media, and even business.

The movement's success with the majority of middle-class women was plain. It tried to attract working-class and racial-minority women, too, but with much less success. The appeal of careers to personally frustrated middle-class women did not touch most working-class women. As one of them said, "A lot of women are much better off married and at home than they would be at some low-paying job, and they know this; they've usually worked before, after all." They saw that kind of work as temporary, and hoped to escape from it someday. For many nonprofessional women, of whatever class, the jobs they could get were rarely interesting or fulfilling.

After four years as head of NOW, Betty stepped down from the presidency. She was divorced and had to go back to writing and lecturing to earn a living. That year—1970—there were about 3000 members of NOW in thirty cities. Although it was a small organization, Betty believed there were a great many more women "out there" ready to take dramatic action for equality. The fiftieth anniversary of the winning of the women's right to vote would fall on August 26. A national Call to a Women's Strike for Equality went out, and feverish preparations began to make it a success. On the chosen day, in New York alone, 50,000 women, many with daughters and grandmothers, marched with pride and joy down Fifth Avenue. In Boston, too, in Baltimore, San Francisco, Miami, often thousands marched. They felt ten feet tall as they showed the world that "sisterhood is powerful." By the mid-1980s NOW had a membership of 250,000.

Often called by the press "the mother of the movement," Betty became a roving ambassador for women's rights. She was invited to speak abroad. Women in many nations wanted to hear how to organize to win their goals. She traveled to France, Sweden, Egypt, Finland, England, India, Israel, Czechoslovakia. She made many cross-country tours of the United States. She taught and did her own research in several uni-

versities. She spoke before all kinds of business, professional, religious, and labor groups. She has served as consultant to foundations and to government commissions.

Betty is now in her sixties, with three grown children and a grandson. Daniel has become a physicist, Jonathan an engineer, Emily a pediatrician. Living in the 1980s in a Manhattan apartment, and at times in a small town on Long Island, she keeps close to her family and her friends. With the birth of her grandson, Rafael, she felt she turned another corner. "There is a delight, a comfort, an easing of the burden, a renewal

of joy in my own life, to feel the stream of life of which I am a part going on like this," she said.

Since *The Feminine Mystique* Betty has published two more books. In 1976 came *It Changed My Life,* a selection of her writings on the women's movement, mixed with her personal memories. In 1981 *The Second Stage* appeared. In it she discussed new questions faced by the young women and men sharing in the first stage of the movement for equality which she had helped to start. The book deals with the problems of combining work, marriage, and children into satisfying lives.

"Women must have the choice to have children without paying for it professionally or politically," Betty wrote in *The Second Stage*. "The fact that women are the people who give birth to children must be taken into account in the conditions of work and in the provisions for parental leave and child care."

Women can have children, can have love, can have their professions if they work out flexible arrangements at home and at work. Don't try to be Superwoman at the office and Supermom at home, she urges. The same goes for men, she adds. The second stage is not a matter for women alone. "Men may be at the cutting edge," she believes. Many men still have to be fought and changed, she knows. But Betty holds that "it is a mistake to assume every man is the enemy, and not to recognize how much men are gearing themselves to change." It will take hard bargaining and lots of persuasion to overcome resistance. But for her, family is the new feminist frontier.

Betty Friedan long ago earned her place in the history of women worldwide. Every book on the struggle for women's rights includes her achievement. When a reporter asked her what she wanted to be remembered for, she replied, "As the one who said women are people." She has shown both men and women that there are better ways to live.

ABOUT THIS BOOK

I met Betty Friedan when we were both working as young journalists in New York City. I saw her a few times in the next years, then lost track of her until she emerged as a leader of the new women's movement. As a historian concerned with the life of my own time, I of course read her path-breaking book, *The Feminine Mystique,* and her articles. Once or twice I heard her speak in public meetings. What she had to say stretched my mind. Men, if they believed in the equality of the sexes, could be feminists, too. I was glad to join in the movement.

When I decided to write this biography, I went to the library to read everything I could find by or about her. I reread her books, *The Feminine Mystique, It Changed My Life,* and *The Second Stage.* I interviewed many people who knew her, from college classmates to friends and co-workers in the women's movement. Then I interviewed Betty herself for several hours.

Finally I visited the Schlesinger Library on the History of Women in America, at Radcliffe College in Cambridge, Massachusetts. There Betty's papers, covering the events and work of a lifetime, are available for research.

This book is the outcome of what I learned. While it sticks to the facts, it cannot help but be influenced by my admiration for a remarkable person.   M.M.

921
FRI   Meltzer, Milton

            Betty Friedan

LOUIS WELCH MIDDLE SCHOOL